D1123673

Monster Museum

MARILYN SINGER
ILLUSTRATIONS BY
GRIS GRIMLY

HYPERION BOOKS FOR CHILDREN
NEW YORK

To monster maven David Lubar
—M.S.

To Charles Addams—
You changed my bright world to the gloomy one I adore.
—G.G.

ACKNOWLEDGMENTS
Many thanks to Steve Aronson, Michele Coppola, Dian Curtis Regan,
my excellent editors, Donna Bray and Shannon Dean, and everyone at Hyperion.
—M.S.

LIBRARY OF CONGRESS CATALOGING-IN-PUBLICATION DATA
Singer, Marilyn.
Monster museum / Marilyn Singer ; illustrations by Gris Grimly.
p. cm.
ISBN 0-7868-0520-X (trade)
1. Monsters—Juvenile poetry. 2. Children's poetry, American.
[1. Monsters—Poetry. 2. American poetry.] I. Grimly, Gris—ill.
II. Title.
PS3569.I546 M6 2001
811'.54—dc21
00-046169

Visit www.hyperionchildrensbooks.com

Exhibits

Monster Museum

Welcome, brave souls, to the Monster Museum!
We've got werewolves and mummies
    (you really must see 'em)
And zombies that dance,
    from a big mausoleum.
We've got spirits and spooks
    that gibber and groan,
A bad-tempered giant
    who's just here on loan

And that Count with sharp fangs
    who is rather well-known.
There's a cool cockatrice
    that's completely obscure,
(You can read all the facts in this lovely brochure)
Plus some creepy surprises—
    of that I am sure!
So, come along, children, and let's start the tour!

Count Dracula

When it comes to monsters having class,
Count Dracula's the winner.
He had style and he had grace,
Not a hair was out of place,
And he dressed up nicely every night
for dinner.

The Werewolf

If you meet a werewolf
   late at night,
Do not invite him for a bite.
Don't question him of his relation
   to a poodle or Dalmatian.
Don't ask him what he does for fun
   If you meet a werewolf,
Scream—
   then run!

The Zombie

Have you seen a zombie samba?
    Have you seen it bunny-hop?
Have you seen it do a polka
    Or that old dance called "the slop"?

Have you seen a zombie hustle?
    Would it tap-dance while you gawk?
Uh-uh, all a zombie ever does
    is do the zombie walk!

Man-eating Plants

Man-eating plants,
Man-eating plants,
   Look out! They're coming to get us.

Man-eating plants,
Man-eating plants,
   Watch out! They look just like lettuce.

Man-eating plants,
Man-eating plants,
   Good grief! They're coming in dozens.

Man-eating plants,
Man-eating plants,
   They're mad 'cause we munched on their cousins.

Man-eating plants,
Man-eating plants,
    They'll take out your brains and your will.

Man-eating plants,
Man-eating plants,
    Your veins will run with chlorophyll!

You'd better not wait
Until it's too late—
    Leave town while you still have the chance.

Leave your tractor and tiller,
But take your weed killer
    'Cause here come those
    man-eating plants!

The Mummy

The mummy's snapped.
She's come unwrapped.
  She's making quite a fuss
'cause someone knocked on,
someone rocked on
  her sarcophagus.

She lays a curse
in ringing verse,
  "By Set and by Osiris!
May your driveway freeze up,
your engine seize up,
  your computer get a virus!"

The raider sighs.
He moans, he cries.
    He begs her to be fair:
"Take my car and my scooter,
but don't wreck my computer
    For I must play Solitaire!"

The raider repents.
The mummy relents:

"Okay, I'll release you from blame."
The raider blinks.
The mummy winks—
    "But you'll have to teach me
    that game."

Amid the gloom
of that dark tomb
    the poor guy will be staying.
He's sealed his fate—
he'll have to wait
    until she gives up playing.

Frankenstein's Monster

They gave me some bolts,
They gave me some jolts.
They gave me a great deal of fame.

They gave me a bride,
And even some pride.
But they never did give me a name.

Mrs. ?

I'm called Frankenstein,
But it's *his* name—not mine.
And the two of us aren't the same.

I'd rather be Bud
Or Wolfgang or Spud,
Or something not nearly so lame

As the handle that stuck—
What a bad piece of luck!
And all of you folks are to blame!

No wonder I'm cranky—
Stop calling me Frankie!
Won't *somebody* give me a name!

Dr. Jekyll and Mr. Hyde

Dr. J: I'm an even-tempered gent,

Mr. H: No, I'm not, no, I'm not.

Dr. J: Though perhaps a trifle bent.

Mr. H: You all rot, you all rot.

Dr. J: All day long I never shirk

Mr. H: All night long I'm wide awake,

Dr. J: From my scientific work.

Mr. H: Looking for more laws to break.

Dr. J: When our little chat is through,

Mr. H: Cut the talk, cut the talk.

Dr. J: I'll imbibe my latest brew.

Mr. H: Time to stalk, time to stalk.

Dr. J: Then, I think you'll cease to heckle—

Mr. H: Come and take a stroll outside

Dr. J: Yours sincerely, Dr. Jekyll.

Mr. H: In the dark with Mr. Hyde.

The Blob

What kind of a job
    would you offer the Blob?
Not butcher nor baker nor cook.
He can't wear an apron,
He'd swallow a patron.
    He'd cover the counter with gook.

What kind of vocation
    would you give this creation?
Not pilot nor plumber nor clerk.
He can't fly a plane,
He'd slide down the drain.
    He'd plop on a shelf or just lurk.

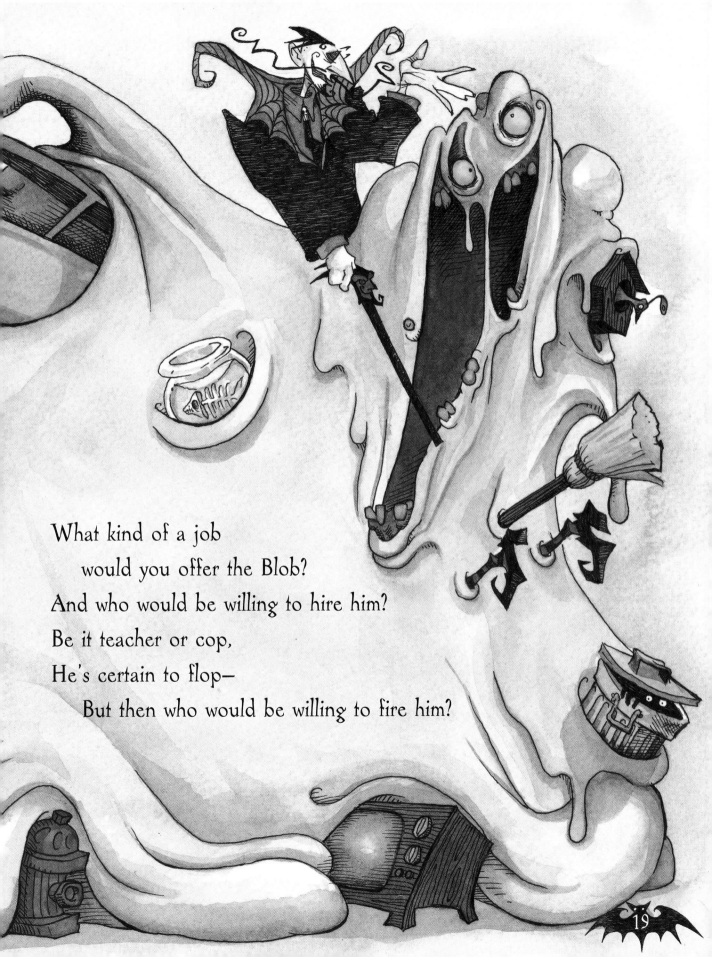

What kind of a job
   would you offer the Blob?
And who would be willing to hire him?
Be it teacher or cop,
He's certain to flop—
   But then who would be willing to fire him?

King Kong

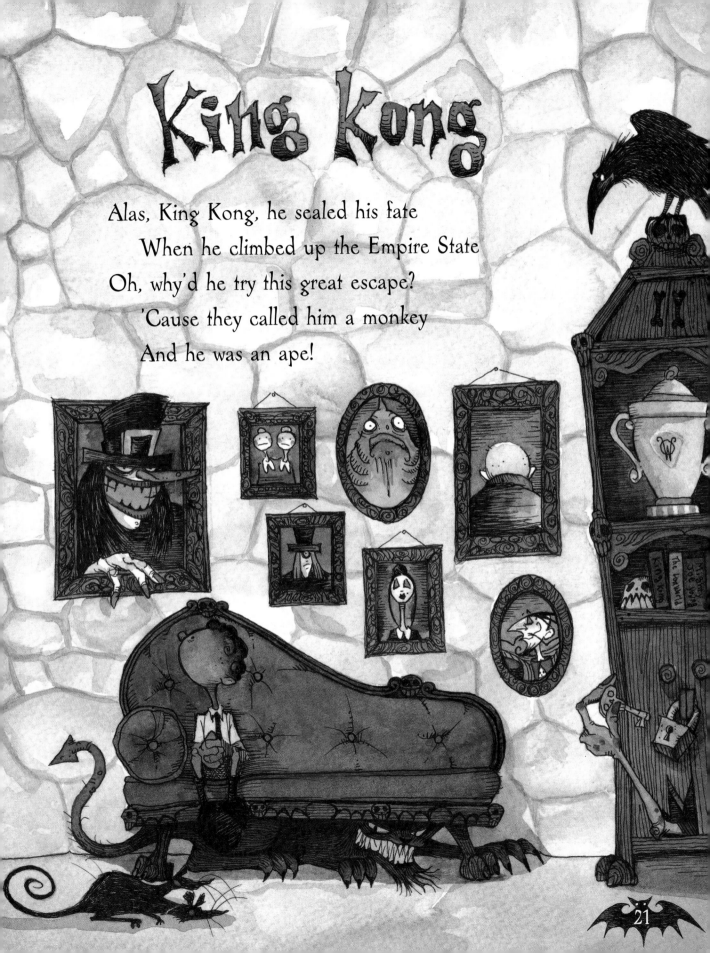

Alas, King Kong, he sealed his fate
    When he climbed up the Empire State
Oh, why'd he try this great escape?
    'Cause they called him a monkey
    And he was an ape!

The Gremlin

Don't get a gremlin for a pet.
It has no sense of etiquette.
A pudding it will swallow whole,
    and then proceed to eat the bowl.

Don't get a gremlin for a pet.
It will invade your TV set,
Put polka dots upon the screen,
    and turn folks' faces blue or green.

Don't get a gremlin for a pet.
It's guaranteed to bite the vet.
So please avoid a big mistake,
    Get something nicer—like a snake.

The Ogre, The Troll

They're two of a kind,
  the ogre, the troll
Though one is so large
  and one is so elfish.
They share the same thoughts
  They have the same goal—
To act really mean
  and totally selfish.

They're two of a kind,
   the ogre, the troll
Though one keeps a castle
   and one blocks a bridge.
They'll get in your face,
   They'll charge you a toll—
Your money, your life
   or the stuff in your fridge.

They're two of a kind,
   the ogre, the troll
Though one likes to slap folks
   and one likes to kick them.
They're the dumbest of dumb
   (and we've taken a poll)
So a goat or a yokel
   could certainly lick them!

The Giant

Acting defiant
to a furious giant
is really a delicate issue
for he's far from petite,
he's got very big feet,
and he might be inclined
just to squish you.

BigFoot

Can you picture Bigfoot's wedding?
Ice-cream cake and lots of sledding,
Every single guest is shedding—
   on this awesome day.

Such a shaggy groom and bride,
Ten feet tall and four feet wide,
Howling while the knot is tied—
   on this awesome day.

Hearts are light and palms are sweaty,
Tossing snowballs like confetti,
When Mister marries Missus Yeti.

What an awesome day!

Medusa

You want to be a millionaire?
   Have gold and jewels beyond compare?
I'll give you wealth
   (can't promise health)
if you will dare
   to do my hair.

1. 2.

            Lately I have such a whim
               to get a perm—or just a trim.
            An antique Greek
               can still look chic.
            A bit more prim—
               but far less grim.

3. 4. 5.

            My ends will never split or break.
               My scalp won't shed a single flake.
            There's just one condition—
               to be my beautician,
            have you got what it takes
               to put curlers on snakes?

The cockatrice and Co.

Those mixed-up beasts from ancient Greece:
The chimera, the cockatrice,
The gorgon and the griffin, too—
Each one of them's a traveling zoo.
Head of lion, wings of eagle—
Is that part snake, or is it beagle?
Which one's breath is bound to grill you?
Which one's looks are sure to kill you?
Keep 'em straight, and you're a hero.
Hesitate, and, zap, you're zero!

The Unicorn

A lizard with wings is a horror,
A stallion with wings is a beaut.
A snake with a horn is a nightmare,
A mare with a horn is just cute.

When we're speaking of things that are scary,
Let's consider the equine clan cursed.
It's reptiles that make the best monsters,
And horses the absolute worst!

Poltergeist

If your sofa's shaking,
If your toilet's quaking,
If your china's flying,
If your walls are sighing,
If your dog gets banished,
If your homework's vanished,
If you hear piano playing,
 Listen, pal, it's time for praying
'Cause your new unwanted boarder
 Thrives on chaos and disorder,
 Stuff to fling and stuff to heist.
Hurry up and get ghost-busted
 Or I promise you'll get dusted
By that ghost known coast to coast
 As a pesky poltergeist.

Ghost

My brother is a poltergeist,
My sister is a bogey.
My mother is a revenant,
My father's an old fogy.
And I am just a little ghost,
My pals all call me Bantam.
I'm hoping to grow long and tall
And change my name to Phantom.

Banshee

'Tis a shame that I left Ireland.
'Tis a crime I left the farm.
　How folks quailed there
　　when I wailed there,
　　　warning them of harm.

'Tis a shame that I left Ireland.
'Tis a crime, this urban sprawl.
　With the honking and the blaring
　　and the whining and the swearing,
　　　not a soul hears a banshee at all!

EXIT
for
those who
Survived!

Bid farewell, brave souls, to
   the Monster Museum!
Our creatures are grand
   (don't you wish you could be 'em?)
And maybe today you've got magic
   to free 'em.
What happens with monsters will always depend
   on how much you know
      and just what you pretend.
Be kind and you'll find
   you'll have one for a friend.

Glos–Scary

BANSHEE: An Irish ghost whose wail says someone's going to die. In a big city, it would be hard to hear a banshee even right outside your door.

BIGFOOT: Called Sasquatch in North America and Yeti in Asia. A huge, hairy, shy creature, Bigfoot prefers mountains, valleys, and cool weather. Many people claim to have seen and even photographed Sasquatch or Yeti (or his footprints), but so far, no one has had a conversation with him.

THE BLOB: A big shapeless movie monster from outer space. It likes to attack small towns. It doesn't seem to have many other talents.

COCKATRICE AND CO.: These Greek monsters are hard to keep straight. They are classically depicted this way:

   Chimera: Lion's head, goat's body, dragon's tail.

   Cockatrice: Snake's body, rooster's head, bat wings.

   Gorgon: Human, with snaky hair, boar's tusks, bird wings, and claws.

   Griffin: Eagle's head and beak, lion's body, snake or scorpion's tail.

COUNT DRACULA: The most famous vampire of all time, he lives in a castle in Transylvania and has starred in more movies than any other monster. Each night he becomes a bat and flies out to find necks to bite and blood to drink. He doesn't do well around daylight, crosses, or garlic. For more information on this bloodsucker, read Bram Stoker's novel DRACULA (1897).

DR. JEKYLL AND MR. HYDE: Smart Dr. Jekyll wanted to study man's dark side. He made up a potion and drank it (several times) to become the evil Mr. Hyde. This case of split personality gave author Robert Louis Stevenson a nightmare, which he documented in THE STRANGE CASE OF DR. JEKYLL AND MR. HYDE (1886).

FRANKENSTEIN'S MONSTER: Dr. Frankenstein put together a monster from the body parts of dead people and brought it to life using electricity. Mary Shelley was the first to write about him in her novel FRANKENSTEIN (1818). Today everyone calls the creature Frankenstein, but the truth is neither Mary nor Dr. F ever gave the poor guy a name.

GHOST: The spirit of a dead person (or an animal). There are many different names for ghosts, including bogey, revenant, and phantom.

GIANT: A creature of enormous size. Giants have been around much longer than people. Some are mean and stupid and like to eat people. Some are kind and particularly friendly to children.

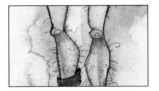

GREMLIN: A mischievous spirit, especially around tools and machinery. Gremlins like to burn your toast, make your shower run cold, and mess up your TV.

KING KONG: Gorillas are usually peaceful animals. But not King Kong. Who can blame him? Being kidnapped from his island home and put on display could drive a mammoth gorilla crazy enough to climb up the Empire State Building with a screaming woman in his hand. So could being called a monkey instead of an ape.

MAN-EATING PLANTS: They're big plants and they eat people. Featured in movies such as THE DAY OF THE TRIFFIDS and LITTLE SHOP OF HORRORS, they're related to little Venus flytraps, which eat bugs.

 **MEDUSA:** A Greek monster with snakes for hair. Medusa was a Gorgon (see COCKATRICE AND CO.) One look at her face and you turn to stone.

MUMMY: The body of a dead person, carefully preserved and wrapped so that it can enter the Egyptian afterlife. This mummy has called on two Egyptian gods to help her—Set, God of Destruction, and Osiris, God of the Underworld.

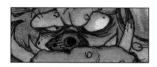 **OGRE:** A big (but not as huge as a giant), bad-tempered, ugly monster that likes to eat people.

POLTERGEIST: An invisible spirit or force that throws your dishes, rattles your doors, and steals your stuff. Poltergeist activity may be caused by a spirit or by an unknowing live person who is angry, but doesn't know how to show it.

 **TROLL:** A short, bad-tempered ugly monster that likes to eat people.

UNICORN: A horse, usually white, with a single horn on its forehead. Many believe the horn has magical powers to heal or to punish the wicked. In the Western world, unicorns are wilder and less easy to tame. In the Eastern world, they have the reputation for being more peaceful and bringing good luck.

 **WEREWOLF:** A person who changes into a wolf at each full moon. Two ways to become a werewolf are to be bitten by one or to be born of werewolf parents. Some folks, however, can become werewolves at will. Like wolves, werewolves need to hunt. Unlike wolves, they'll hunt people.

ZOMBIE: A body without a soul. In the African-Caribbean practice of Voodoo, a zombie can be created and controlled by a powerful sorceror. In American movies zombies are famous for their nasty habit of eating people and for the weird way they walk.